Thanksgiving Is Here!

by Diane Goode

HARPERCOLLINSPUBLISHERS

For Peter

Thanksgiving Is Here!
Copyright © 2003 by Diane Goode
For information address HarperCollins Children's Books,
a division of HarperCollins Publishers, 1350 Avenue of the
Americas, New York, NY 10019.
www.harperchildrens.com

Library of Congress Cataloging-in-Publication Data
Goode, Diane.
Thanksgiving is here! / by Diane Goode.— 1st ed.
        p.   cm.
Summary: A family gathers to celebrate Thanksgiving at
Grandma's house.
ISBN 0-06-051588-0 — ISBN 0-06-051589-9 (lib. bdg.)
ISBN 0-06-051590-2 (pbk.)
[1. Thanksgiving Day—Fiction.   2. Family life—Fiction.]
I. Title.
PZ7 .G604 Th   2003   2002151781
[E]—dc21

Typography by Elynn Cohen
❖

When the sun comes up at Grandma's house . . .

the Thanksgiving turkey goes in the oven . . . and then the doorbell rings.

DINGDONG! Open up, Grandma! It's me, Maggie . . . and Peter . . . and Mom and Pop and baby Jack.

We've all come to help at Thanksgiving.

We peel the potatoes and roll out the dough.

We all love to cook at Thanksgiving.

DINGDONG! The cousins have come. They brought the new baby . . .

. . . but whose dog is that? Come in. Come in!

The sofa goes here and the piano goes there.   DINGDONG!

We need lots of room at Thanksgiving.

DINGDONG!
DINGDONG!

Look who's back.

MORE uncles and aunts, cousins and friends.

They all push and drag the tables and chairs.

We need a BIG table at Thanksgiving.

At Grandma's house the chairs don't match . . . but we don't mind.

We all have a place at the table.

YACKETY-YAK! At Grandma's house we all kick back. WAH, WAH!

It sounds like someone is hungry.

In the kitchen cranberries pop and corn cakes sizzle.

We all love Grandma's cooking.

At Grandma's house we wait for the dinner bell.

DING-A-LING!

DING-A-LING! Grandma rings. Everyone come to the table!

Thanksgiving dinner is ready.

At Grandma's house we all give thanks . . .

unfold our napkins . . .

. . . and EAT!

We pass the corn cakes and spoon on the gravy . . . mmmmmm!

We eat till we're full at Thanksgiving.

At Grandma's house we help clear the table.

We all wash and dry at Thanksgiving.

At Grandma's house we can take off our shoes . . . aaaah!

Or . . .

... walk around the block ...

... CLICKETY-CLAK!

Then we all sit and chat . . .YACKETY-YAK! Until . . .

Grandma rings again. *DING-A-LING!*

Everyone back to the table!

Oooh! My favorite . . . pumpkin pie . . .

...and music—ZING, ZING, ZING!—of course.

At Grandma's house we're never too full for dessert.

We've all had a happy Thanksgiving.

When the sun goes down . . .

. . . we get our coats . . .

. . . and kiss good-bye.

And we don't cry, because EVERYONE's going home.

Thank you, Grandma.

Don't worry, Grandpa. . . .

We'll be back.